For Pongi and her bears,
Peanut and Kabuki

Clarion Books
a Houghton Mifflin Company imprint
215 Park Avenue South, New York, NY 10003
Text and illustrations copyright © 1997 by Lydia Dabcovich

The illustrations for this book were executed in gouache on Fabriano Hot Press watercolor paper.
The text is set in 18/23-point Dante.

Printed in the USA

Library of Congress Cataloging-in-Publication Data

Dabcovich, Lydia.
The polar bear son : an Inuit tale / retold and illustrated by Lydia Dabcovich.
    p.   cm.
Summary: An old woman adopts and raises a polar bear cub which grows up and provides for her
even after she has to send it away to save it from the jealous men of the village.
ISBN 0-395-72766-9 PA ISBN 0-395-97567-0
1. Inuit—Folklore. 2. Tales—Arctic regions. [1. Inuit—Folklore. 2. Eskimos—Folklore.
3. Folklore—Arctic regions.] I. Title.
E99.E7D28   1997
398.24'52974446'089971—dc20
    [E]   96-4780
              CIP
              AC
BVG 10 9 8 7 6 5 4

THE POLAR BEAR SON

AN INUIT TALE

RETOLD AND ILLUSTRATED BY LYDIA DABCOVICH

ork

WAY UP NORTH, all alone in a little hut at the edge of an Inuit village, there lived an old woman. She had no family, no strong sons to hunt for her.

The old woman tried to fend for herself by fishing and gathering seeds and berries. But often she was unsuccessful and had to depend on her neighbors for food.

One day, out on the ice, the old woman found a little white polar bear cub. His mother must have been killed, the old woman thought.

So she took him home.

Back in her hut, the old woman fed the cub,
sharing with him the little food she had.
"I will call you Kunikdjuaq," she said.
"Kunikdjuaq, my son."

13

Kunikdjuaq was happy with the old woman.
He was a friendly, round, and fluffy little bear,
and the children of the village loved to play with
him, tumbling about and sliding on the snow.

Spring, summer, and long dark winter passed. Kunikdjuaq grew quickly. When spring came again, he was big and strong enough to go hunting and fishing for the old woman.

Soon the old woman had plenty of meat and fish to eat, furs to keep her warm, and blubber for cooking. And, as is the custom of the Inuit, she shared every good catch with the bear and the whole village.

"Come," called the old woman proudly. "There's more than enough for all of us."

The villagers took the food but, in time, the hunters grew angry because Kunikdjuaq was much better at hunting than they were. And they were jealous that the old woman had found such a good provider.

They decided to kill Kunikdjuaq. But the children overheard the hunters' plan and ran to warn the old woman.

The old woman went from house to house, pleading with the villagers to spare her clever young bear.

"Kunikdjuaq is my son," she said. "Do not take him away from me!"

"This bear is getting too big and strong. He is dangerous," they said. "We will kill him tomorrow. He will make a fine feast for the village, and his fur will keep us warm."

The old woman rushed back home. She told Kunikdjuaq
that he had to leave at once.

"Go," she said. "Go quickly and do not come back."
Crying bitterly, she begged him not to forget her.

25

So Kunikdjuaq left.
Sadly, the old woman and the children
watched him disappear into the distance.

Now the old woman was alone again. From time to time, when she felt very lonely and hungry, she left her hut early in the morning and went very far out on the ice.

Then she called, "Kunikdjuaq! Kunikdjuaq, my son!"

She did not have to wait long before a big polar bear came running to meet her.

It was Kunikdjuaq—
big and strong and sleek and glossy!

The old woman always looked him over carefully, making sure that he had not been injured. Then Kunikdjuaq brought her salmon and seal. They ate some of it together, and the old woman took the rest home with her.

This went on for many years. And, up to this day, the Inuit tell the story of the faithful bear Kunikdjuaq and the old woman who brought him up.

AUTHOR'S NOTE

The word *Inuit* means "the people" in the Inuit language. For thousands of years many tribes of Inuit have lived throughout the vast, cold, and forbidding Arctic region, from eastern Siberia and the western coast of the Pacific to Greenland and the eastern Atlantic shores of Canada.

In their harsh environment the Inuit survived by hunting and fishing. They lived in small communities, often traveling together and sharing their catches as they followed animals, fish, and birds during seasonal migrations. Game was frequently scarce, but when and where it was available, the Inuit hunted whales, walruses, and seals; caribou, polar bears, and musk oxen; wolves, foxes, squirrels, hares, weasels, and various land and water birds; and they fished for salmon, Arctic char, pike, and whitefish. In some areas they gathered roots and berries during the short summer.

The captured animals provided meat; skins and pelts to be made into clothes, boots, tents, and kayaks; sinews for threads and ropes; bones to be made into weapons and tools; and oil for stone stoves and lamps. The hunters believed that powerful spirits sent them the game they depended upon, and they thanked every animal they killed for allowing itself to be caught.

The Inuit lived in a variety of dwellings. Igloos made out of blocks of ice and skin tents provided shelter during long hunting trips. Sod and stone houses were used for more permanent settlements. With the arrival of European and American explorers and traders, villages of wooden huts developed near trading posts. At the same time, metal tools and utensils, guns, kerosene stoves and lamps, and textiles such as cotton, wool, and canvas were introduced. Nowadays the Inuit live in permanent settlements, many in prefabricated houses.

During the long, dark winters the Inuit liked to play games and tell stories. There were many tales of powerful animals, strong hunters, and supernatural beings. The story of the polar bear son Kunikdjuaq (pronounced *koo-nick-joo-uck*) was told in various areas of the Arctic and collected by anthropologists.

This adaptation is based on *The Bear Story*, collected and transcribed by Frans Boas for *Central Eskimo* (*Annual Report of American Ethnology, Vol. VI*, Washington, 1888), retold in *Eskimomarchen* (Berlin: Axel Juncker Verlag, 1924, and Frankfurt: Insel Verlag, 1984), and on *Kunikdjuaq*, written for children by Maria Leach, who included it in *The Rainbow Book of American Folktales* (Cleveland and New York: World Publishing Co., 1958).

The Polar Bear Son includes elements from the various versions of the story. In my illustrations I have tried to convey a mythical feeling, inspired by the simple and powerful shapes of Inuit sculpture, and to render the awesome beauty and vast space of the Arctic landscape.